Samuel French Acting Edition

No One Is Forgotten

by Winter Miller

FOR PRODUCTION ENQUIRIES

UNITED STATES AND CANADA
info@concordtheatricals.com
1-866-979-0447

UNITED KINGDOM AND EUROPE
licensing@concordtheatricals.co.uk
020-7054-7200

Each title is subject to availability from Concord Theatricals Corp., depending upon country of performance. Please be aware that *NO ONE IS FORGOTTEN* may not be licensed by Concord Theatricals Corp. in your territory. Professional and amateur producers should contact the nearest Concord Theatricals Corp. office or licensing partner to verify availability.

be invented, including mechanical, electronic, photocopying, recording, videotaping, or otherwise, without the prior written permission of the publisher. No one shall upload this title(s), or part of this title(s), to any social media websites.

For all enquiries regarding motion picture, television, and other media rights, please contact Concord Theatricals Corp.

MUSIC USE NOTE

Licensees are solely responsible for obtaining formal written permission from copyright owners to use copyrighted music in the performance of this play and are strongly cautioned to do so. If no such permission is obtained by the licensee, then the licensee must use only original music that the licensee owns and controls. Licensees are solely responsible and liable for all music clearances and shall indemnify the copyright owners of the play(s) and their licensing agent, Concord Theatricals Corp., against any costs, expenses, losses and liabilities arising from the use of music by licensees. Please contact the appropriate music licensing authority in your territory for the rights to any incidental music.

IMPORTANT BILLING AND CREDIT REQUIREMENTS

If you have obtained performance rights to this title, please refer to your licensing agreement for important billing and credit requirements.

NO ONE IS FORGOTTEN was presented by winter miller's community theater, in association with Kathleen and Henry Chalfant, Angelina Fiordelisi, Kelli Giddish, Kristin and James Hatt, Tom Marshall and Kathy Keneally, Susan Miller and Lida Orzeck, and Naka Nathaniel at the Rattlestick Playwrights Theater in New York, New York on July 8, 2019.

The performance was directed by Winter Miller, with sets by Meredith Ries, lights by Stacey DeRosier, sound by Tyler Kieffer, costumes and props by Rhys Roffey, and fight choreography by Rocío Mendez, and intimacy consulting by Katie Pearl. The production stage manager and production manager was Wednesday Sue Derrico, the assistant stage manager was Jackie Rivera, the technical director was Lory Henning, and the assistant director was Emily Welty.

It was co-produced by Amanda Cooper, and the associate producer was Shannon Musgrave, and the assistant producer was Zoe Senese-Grossberg. The cast was as follows:

LALI. . . . . Sarah Nina Hayon
BENG . . . . Renata Friedman

NO ONE IS FORGOTTEN was part of Rattlestick's curated rental program, and was a New Georges Supported Production. It received developmental support from The Magic Theatre, Labyrinth Theater Company, New York Stage & Film, The Lark, Salt Lake Acting Company, Unicorn Theatre, and was presented at the 2017 NNPN National Showcase of New Plays.

CHARACTERS

LALI – over thirty-five, a person of color, a woman, an aid worker.
BENG – over thirty-five, any race, a woman, a reporter.

SETTING

A small, entirely bare room in an unknown place.

TIME

Present.

ELEMENTS OF STYLE

Notes on punctuation and language.

(.)	A period marks an end of a sentence, but keep it moving. Your thoughts flow easily into the next thought.
(–)	A dash indicates a thought suddenly interrupted.
(/)	At a slash, the next speaker interrupts the first speaker's line. An overlap.
(…)	Ellipses are a very brief pause. Don't settle in, take a breath and go on.
(Pause.)	If you don't know what to say or you're weighing your response.
(Silence.)	Non-verbal standoff, ranging from awkward to menacing. A silence between two people comfortable together.
(Beat.)	Wait. A revelation. Once the thought takes hold, speak.

PRODUCTION NOTES

Lali and Beng are cis-women. To cast otherwise, please request permission. Four actors could play in rep, rotating pairs nightly.

Pacing is such that scenes begin abruptly and may conclude without a resolution.

The amount of light in the cell never waivers, it is dim and there is no sense of day or night.

The only ambient noise is specifically indicated in the text. The soundscape during scenes is ambiguous. At times the prisoners may hear noises beyond their cell, such as a generator, a buzzing, something wheeled past, maybe a faint beeping or mechanical vibration, maybe wind, someone walking by who could be holding keys, possibly furniture being moved or dragged, maybe the sound of a dog barking, maybe the thud or bump of wood or steel. Most sounds are not clearly identifiable, and the prisoners may also imagine sounds.

Transitions between scenes are tiny scenes unto themselves; they indicate the passage of time. The quality of light and sound must reflect an entirely different and changing universe from the monotony of the lights in their cell. Sound and light are dynamic and specific to the transitions. There is definitely no sonic spill from transition into scenes.

Avoid staging the pissing in the bucket and the sex scenes gratuitously. Less really is more. Nudity in a small space is most often a distraction for an audience, particularly for a long period of time, like at the end.

The prisoners wear shapeless, worn, billowy cotton unisex shifts that slip over their heads. They are barefoot, unshaven and unclean. Underneath, the actors may wear men's worn boxer briefs, as if that is what they've been handed when their own wore out. They may be wearing athletic-type bras, (no lace, no underwire) something they were wearing in the field when they were taken, that has lost some elasticity but it's all they have. Their shifts are long enough on their body that even during sex, the audience need never see anything that discomforts the actors. Particularly in the first sex scene, their removal of boxers should seem pretty banal. Most things that they do in the cell they have done hundreds of times before, so in moments when they do surprise each other, there is delight in the novelty of the unexpected.

Besides the fear of possible danger or abuse, when they are not meditating or engaged in some form of escapism, things are very, very boring. By this time in their captivity, there are relatively few stories they haven't already spoken or heard.

The stage is surrounded by audience on all four sides, there may be the suggestion of a wall, but there are none. The captives are fully exposed.

Any visible surfaces of the cell are a mix of concrete, linoleum, or worn carpet. There is no window, nor a light. The door has a transom at the bottom, four inches by ten inches. It slides open and closed when the bowl and water are pushed in. The water bottle holds minimum sixteen ounces as it's highly unlikely to find small water bottles in many parts of the world. Oatmeal has a nice consistency for the rice glop they are served. Actors will disappear through a trap door during transitions; this is magical and mysterious. In a proscenium, aim for the effect of there's nowhere for anyone to escape, not the captives, not the audience, we're in this together.

Никто не забыт, и ничто не забыто

Nikto ne zabyt, i nichto ne zabyto

Nobody is forgotten, and nothing is forgotten

– "Here Lie Leningraders," Olga Berggoltz, Russian Poet,
inscribed on the wall at Piskarevskoe Memorial Cemetery,
St. Petersburg, Russia

For those who returned and those who could not.
For the Foley and Pearl families.
For Albert, Anna, Corky and Mark.

Scene One

(**LALI** *and* **BENG** *are in a small, bare room
without windows or light. The floor is worn
down carpet and linoleum. The door is just
a suggestion, but at bottom is an eight inch-
high transom that slides open when their
bowl of food is shoved in or removed. In one
corner is a bucket for waste.)*

*(The captives are barefoot and unclean,
dressed in worn, flimsy cotton shifts.)*

*(They are playing hangman without paper
or pen.)*

LALI. Four letters.

BENG. S.

LALI. No.

BENG. R.

LALI. No.

BENG. E.

LALI. No.

BENG. A.

LALI. No.

BENG. *(Reviewing.)* S R E A... *(Thinks.)* K.

LALI. No.

BENG.	**LALI.**
T,	No,
O,	No,
I,	No,
U,	No,

BENG. What the fuck? Is this English?

LALI. Yes.

BENG. It has no vowels!

LALI. *(Shrugs.)* You're the wordsmith...

    (She counts out four fingers at **BENG.***)*

Four letters.

BENG. *(Smug.)* Atrophy.

LALI. You're one guess away from hanging.
    (Gleefully.) I'll add fingers.

BENG. Y.

LALI. Oooh!

BENG. L.

LALI. Good!

BENG. X.

LALI. Yes...

BENG. P!

LALI. No P!

BENG. D, V, H

LALI. Look, it's four fucking letters and you have Y L X.
    (Providing an ordered clue.) L ...Y ...and... X...

        *(***BENG*** begins to do pushups, probably four to six.)*

        *(***LALI*** makes a victorious "air" notch and does two or three pushups.)*

BENG. Fruits my mom likes.

LALI. Does this include dried?

BENG. Oh Jeannette is a *big* fan of dried fruit. Never leaves home without it.

LALI. Okay. Mango, prune, apricot, pineapple, green melon, cantaloupe, grape, peach, nectarine. Want me to keep going?

BENG. Oui, madame. Mais bien sûr.

        (During **LALI***'s new list,* **BENG** *barks "Repeat" immediately after* **LALI** *repeats a fruit she's*

mentioned above, such as peach, grape, apricot, but **LALI** *ignores her and continues to list.)*

LALI. Peach, / pear, apple,

BENG. Repeat!

LALI. grape, / blueberry, cranberry, orange,

BENG. Repeat!

LALI. banana, apricot, / tomato,

BENG. Repeat!

LALI. papaya. Kiwi. Plum.

BENG. That's it? Guava, tangerine / lemon –

LALI. *(Buzzer noise.)* I said tangerine.

BENG. You said nectarine!

LALI. I said both.

BENG. Admit you're / wrong.

LALI. I'm not wrong, / you are.

BENG. TANGELO, STAR FRUIT, lime, papaya / coconut –

LALI. *(Buzzer noise.)* I said papaya. I definitely did.

(Pause. Silence.)

Kings:

BENG. *(A sigh.)* Arthur, Charles 1, 2, Leopold, George 1, 2, 3, 4, Henry 1, 2, 3, 4, 5, 6, 7, 8… Olaf, Sebastian, Phillip, Taksin,

> *(***LALI*** *lifts her shift to piss in the bucket as* **BENG** *continues to list.)*

Ferdinand… Harald 1, 2, 3, 4, 5, Robert the Bruce, James Nicholas…

LALI. Richard, Alexander, Malcolm, Sebastian the Asleep, Ivan –

BENG. *(Gesturing to* **LALI***, imitating her.) Lali* the Smug

LALI. Ivan the Red. Ivan the / Terrible.

BENG. *Lali* the Know-It- / All

LALI. Yuri the Long Hands –

BENG. *Lali* the SAVIOR OF HUMANITY.

LALI. Vasily the Dark, Robert the Lame King –

BENG. *(With a sudden toe cramp.)* Agh.

        (BENG *tends to her toe. Pause.)*

LALI. Is it a pinch, or steady dull?

BENG. Like a vise.

LALI. …Cramp.

BENG. Mmmhmmmn.

LALI. *(Interested.)* Inside, deep? Or, surface.

BENG. Surface.

LALI. Ah… *(Thinks.)*

BENG. Agh.

LALI. *(Concluding.)* Yehhh, you need a banana.

BENG. *(Pleased.)* Great.

LALI. Want me to run out and get you one?

BENG. No, I'm going to the store later, pick up a bunch of stuff.

LALI. Cool, cool… Get me some Wite-Out? And beans and franks? Popovers, nachos.

BENG I'm getting sausage, taco shells, ice cream sandwiches, dates, hand sanitizer, detergent, pampers, what else?

LALI. *(Amused.)* Pampers…

BENG. Well. If people stop by with a baby. It's nice to offer.

LALI. Of course, some almonds or chips too. We're out of TP, Band-Aids, dog food, we need a new bottle brush, nail polish –

BENG. Want me to get nail polish remover and those cotton things too?

LALI. Sure, why not? Oh! Fishsticks, frozen. OJ fresh, *with* pulp.

BENG. I should get oranges and squeeze it fresh.

LALI. *(Pleased.)* You spoil us.

BENG. Can't help it can I? You care what kind of sponge I get?

LALI. Nope. *(Thinks.)* But get two colors, so we can tell which is for countertops. Super tampons, or plus, whatever's on sale, and regular. Get shrimp. Squid. Oh, Woolite. Should I just come with you?

BENG. No, you rest. Almost forgot Himalayan sea salt!

LALI. I like rose salt. Ketchup –

BENG. We have an excess of ketchup. Baaacon.

LALI. Get the organic one.

BENG. It's soo expensive.

LALI. Then don't get it at all. Licorice.

BENG. Liver.

LALI. Microwave popcorn.

BENG. *(Delighted by this.)* Mrs. Dash.

LALI. Two pomegranates if they have / them.

BENG. They will. Definitely.

Scene Two

(Faint sound of a generator, maybe.)

(Nothing is going on.)

*(**BENG** and **LALI** are eating a rice glop from the same bowl with their hands. They are hungry but they do not gulp it down.)*

(The sound of something with ineffective wheels dragging outside their room down a hallway.)

(When they finish eating, one of them pushes the bowl up to the transom.)

Scene Three

(The bowl is gone.)

(Eyes closed, they sit anywhere, perhaps at opposite ends.)

BENG. Something narrow…

LALI. *(Thinks.)* Concern.

BENG. No. Something oblong.

LALI. Anxiety.

BENG. Nope.

(Pause, as she thinks of the next clue.)

I spy, with my little eye, something brittle.

*(**LALI** thinks. She makes that clicking sound with her tongue on the roof of her mouth that comes from tapping.)*

LALI. A sand – no – uhhhh – I need a hint.

BENG. One.

LALI. That's the hint? One?

BENG. One hint.

LALI. Oh. Is it a tangible, a locatable thing?

BENG. Maybe.

LALI. It's got to be yes or no.

I'm asking a different question then.

BENG. But maybe is a proper answer.

LALI. It's not a clue.

BENG. Yes it is.

LALI. How?

BENG. Because maybe it is a tangible, locatable thing and maybe it's not.

(One or both may remain in place or roam.)

LALI. I get a new question.

BENG. It's kind of cheating. But go ahead.

LALI. Narrow, oblong, brittle.

BENG. Yes.

LALI. Is it an organ in the upper third of the body?

BENG. No.

LALI. No it's not an organ or no it's not an organ in the upper third of the body?

BENG. You only got one question.

LALI. I'm not closer to guessing it though.

BENG. You can forfeit.

LALI. Fine.

BENG. So you forfeit.

LALI. Another clue.

BENG. Murky, gray. That's two.

LALI. Narrow, oblong, brittle, murky, gray. *(Thinks.)* Fear.

BENG. Congratulations.

But I did have to give you five clues and you asked three questions.

I'm not sure that's a legitimate point.

LALI. It's worth half.

BENG. Nah, you can have the whole point, what the hell.

LALI. No, half is fine. It's fair.

BENG. Just take the whole point.

LALI. No.

BENG. I'm giving you the point, just say thanks and go.

LALI. I don't need charity.

BENG. It's not –

LALI. Half a point.

BENG. Just. Take. It.

LALI. Fine. No point. You're up by three. Right?

BENG. *(Kind of gloating a little.)* Yup. But I'm sure you'll catch me.

> *(**LALI** opens her eyes and looks at **BENG** whose eyes remain closed.)*

> (**LALI** *brushes her hand tenderly across* **BENG***'s chin, a sweet, brief caress along her face.*)

> (**BENG** *opens her eyes. Pleasure.*)

(*Sweetly.*) What's that for?

LALI. It's a precursor...

BENG. (*Beguiled.*) To what?

> (**LALI** *playfully – not hard – gives a mildly aggressive tap to* **BENG***'s chin or cheek.*)

> (**BENG** *observes* **LALI***.*)

> (*Beat.*)

> (**LALI** *closes her eyes.*)

> (**BENG** *looks at her a moment longer and closes her eyes.*)

> (*They resume the game.*)

LALI. I spy with my little eye... Something red.

BENG. Red. Huh... Aorta.

LALI. (*Triumphant.*) No.

BENG. Capillaries.

LALI. (*Triumphant.*) Nope.

BENG. Hint.

LALI. Saw-toothed.

BENG. Red, saw-toothed. Oh! Gum by a molar.

LALI. (*Very triumphant.*) Sorry.

BENG. Not aorta, not capillaries, not gum by a molar. Infected molar is what I mean.

LALI. Still no. But I won't count that as a guess.

BENG. It wasn't, I was clarifying. I get another hint.

LALI. Jowly.

BENG. Jowly?

LALI. Jowly.

BENG. I'm opening my eyes.

> *(They open their eyes.)*

What is "jowly"?

> *(**LALI** makes a jowly face.)*

(Unconvinced.) Okay.

> *(They adjust their positions, now closer and sitting across from each other with legs crossed, knees touching and their eyes closed.)*

Is it...is it...envy?

LALI. Oooooh! Close!

BENG. Shit.

LALI. Kind of close. You can have one more guess.

BENG. Uhm, rejection.

LALI. Fuck! Yes.

BENG. Red, saw-toothed, jowly... Nice.

> *(Beat.)*

> *(**LALI** shifts her whole body – her eyes still closed – and puts her head in **BENG**'s lap, curled up before her.)*

> *(**BENG** tenderly rests a hand on **LALI**'s shoulder.)*

Scene Four

(*A long beat. They are in their own worlds.*)

BENG. You're supposed to be able to open your jaw like a chest of drawers.

(**BENG** *demonstrates a clean jaw opening.*)

Not side to side at all. Mine's making a sound...
Like the tiniest car door closing on a sweatshirt.

(**BENG** *listens, she opens and closes her jaw. It doesn't make the sound, does it? She opens and closes it again.*)

That time it did! Could you hear it?

(*Thoughts elsewhere,* **LALI** *shakes her head no.*)

(**BENG** *opens and closes her jaw.*)

LALI. I heard it! So loud!

BENG. Was it? (*Realizing.*) You're teasing.

LALI. No! It sounded like the tiniest car door / closing on a noodle.

BENG. Shadddddup. Not a noodle. Sweatshirt.

LALI. Do it again.

(**BENG** *opens and closes her jaw.*)

Yes. That is unmistakably the sound of a Mazda Miata slamming on a blue hoodie.

(**BENG** *is amused by Mazda Miata. She places* **LALI**'s *hand against her jaw to feel it.*)

(**LALI** *grazes* **BENG**'s *face with a gesture of tenderness, which means more to* **BENG**.)

Your face is nice.

BENG. With all these spa treatments...

(**LALI** *looks at her and smiles.*)

LALI. Just say thanks.

BENG. Thanks.

    (Pause.)

    (Apropos of nothing, but in reference to a previous conversation.)

You thought I was aloof.

LALI. That actually bothered you...?

BENG. I was surprised, I guess. You never mentioned that.

LALI. What I actually said was, you seemed guarded. Which is no big deal. Is normal.

BENG. That's not how other people have described me. You said I was very nice on the flight, about how I gave you my neck pillow.

LALI. On the plane you *were* very gracious. I was talking about a couple years later when I saw you at the Radisson lounge in N'Djamena. You were engrossed in all the fuss around you. / You had a gaggle.

BENG. There wasn't fuss – those were stringers. I'm sure I wanted to slip away and nurse my Glenlivet in peace.

LALI. They were like twenty-three and *hanging* on your every word.

BENG. That's a rite of passage – everybody has a field crush.

LALI. And you were theirs.

BENG. I'm not saying that... But maybe.

LALI. Who was yours?

BENG. Oh. Ha! Have I never mentioned Carmen Perlez? The James Bond of correspondents – everyone crushed on her. First time I saw her, Kampala, 2008, someone's birthday, people are shit-faced... I step out to smoke... there's Perlez on her satphone, calmly requesting *"a humvee, a bulletproof vest"* – with that accent.
"I'll need a humvee, bulletproof vest, Italian loafers, a silk scarf, an adolescent jag-u-ar...and a helmet. By sunup, please."
Fearless... I was freelance, no idea where to get a fixer, she hooked me up, gave me pointers...

LALI. Was she really attractive?

BENG. Newspaper-sexy: Mystique and Pulitzers.

LALI. And your big crush became your mentor? Smooth.

BENG. No. It wasn't like that.

LALI. Look at you!

BENG. So who was yours?

LALI. Mine would have to be this guy, Uzoma Igwe, a program director with WHO. Really handsome, funny, smart, warm…

BENG. Torrid affair?

LALI. Sadly no. I wouldn't have minded but I wasn't his type. He liked blondes.

BENG. His loss.

> (*An awkward silence.* BENG *looks at* LALI *who does not look at her.*)

> (*Beat.*)

LALI. Given circumstances: No money, no job: Do you / go for pitbull –

BENG. Do I live in a city or a village?

LALI. Doesn't matter, not relevant.

BENG. It's probably easier to be jobless in a village.
Do I have family near? Do we get along?
If I needed to live with them until I got back on my feet, could I?

LALI. (*Patiently.*) Not the question. Pitbull fighting or breeding?

BENG. (*Happily.*) Breeding.

LALI. Fighting. More money, you can only breed every eight to twelve weeks best.

BENG. It's illegal.

LALI. They run the fights out of sight.

BENG. You could lose your bets.

LALI. Not if you train them well.

BENG. (*Pleased.*) Puppies.

(Kind of a draw, each thinks she probably won the point. Not that there's a scoreboard.)

(Pause.)

(New thought.) AIDS or Ebola?

LALI. AIDS 1980s or AIDS now?

BENG. 1980s AIDS. 2014 Ebola.

LALI. Shit... AIDS.

BENG. Yeh. AIDS. ...Liberia, that was... The smell *(Putrid.)*. ...You were or weren't there?

LALI. I was there in... 20... 12. Ebola was 2014. Right?
– Oh, yeah, I had just started with Oxfam in Bukavu.

BENG. Ahhh, yes at Panzi.

LALI. *(Nods.)* God I love Panzi.
...Hey, in Liberia did you run into this guy named Paul, uhhhm. Jesus Christ we're going to forget our fucking names next. *(Delighted.)* Remy! He wrote for The Atlantic or Harper's, one of those...

BENG. Paul Remy. *(Considers.)* Doesn't ring a bell. But *(Shrugs, as in, maybe never met him or maybe my memory is messed up.)* ...

LALI. *(They spent a fun evening together.)* His eyes were turquoise. I've never seen eyes like that. You'd remember him. *(Thinks.)* Why did I bring him up?

BENG. I don't know. Did he have Ebola?

LALI. No. *(Now downplaying the night.)* He was kind of a bag of douche. I borrowed his phone, and he propositioned me. Like we were Bonobos: I used his satphone, therefore clearly I would fuck him.

BENG. And?

LALI. 100%. But, it was right after Mac broke up with me and he'd gone over to Unicef – some cush gig in... Geneva? So, I sowed my oats like a good cliché. *(Shrugs.)*

BENG. I'd have been a good Bonobo. They're so smart to make everything so simple. Eat, barter, fuck, fight, sleep. *(Considers.)* Like us. We don't barter.

(They sit in silence.)

LALI. Is it my go?

BENG. Mine was AIDS or Ebola.

LALI. Co-lo-rec-tal cancer or leukemia?

BENG. Advanced?

LALI. *(Sarcastic.)* No, benign.

BENG. Well, it would matter.

LALI. Indeed.

BENG. Okay, leukemia.

LALI. Colorectal. ...Is it cahler-ectal? Coal-er? Cuhlerectal. It all sounds weird.

BENG. *(Shrugs.)* I'd just want to die quickly. No shitbag and all that.

LALI. Shitbag. *(Shaking her head.)* I had a professor who had a colostomy bag. He talked about it. To the class. It was an ordeal. For him.

BENG. Did it smell? Please tell me it didn't.

LALI. They're made with strong plastic. Besides, it's not like I was in his lap – he was at his desk.

(Pause.)

BENG. I couldn't do the bag. *(Pause.)* I'd end it.

LALI. *(A non-sequitor, from "end it," now thinking about their loved ones.)* The *not* knowing... They can't move on...

BENG. Or they've given up. ...I mean... *(Shrugs.)*

LALI. *(If you were them.)* How long would you wait?

BENG. Before giving up?

LALI. If there was no word...

BENG. I guess I'd like to think...as long as is healthy.

LALI. How would you determine that?

BENG. I don't know. Five years? Seven?

LALI. I don't think I could... Not indefinitely, not without proof...
Even a shred.

> *(They are silent, separate.)*

> *(A beat.)*

> *(They are waiting or not waiting.)*

> *(Muffled sounds from beyond their room. Just some noise?)*

> *(**BENG** and **LALI** listen. They wonder if it might be a beating? Screaming? Moving furniture?)*

> *(Beat.)*

> *(Another sound.)*

BENG. See? That *is* higher pitched.

> *(Pause.)*

Or, it could be the wind.

LALI. I doubt it's the wind.

Scene Five

*(Silently, **LALI** and **BENG** are mid-fuck. They face one another, assertively in a full-bodied embrace. They treat sex as a need, like eating, sleeping, defecating.)*

(This moment is not one of leisured discovery or eroticism, and shouldn't be played for an audience's gaze.)

(They are interrupted well before climax when the transom slides open. They move apart. It's not likely the door will open – but you never know.)

(A bowl of food and a sixteen ounce water bottle three quarters filled with water are deposited through the transom.)

BENG. *(Absurdly pleased.)* Room service!

LALI. *(Joining.)* Oh look, champagne with dinner.

> *(**LALI** reaches for the water and gulps it and passes it to **BENG**.)*
>
> *(Unhurriedly, **BENG** reaches for the bowl.)*
>
> *(They remain reclined, eating with their hands languorously, like emperors.)*

(A post-coital levity, existence is meaningless.) Cumin.

BENG. See, I would flavor it with cardamom, bake it in a dal. With warm chapatis.

LALI. Nice. I'd do…a basil, sage, thyme, rosemary rub, let it marinate overnight. Slow cook for four hours.

BENG. Or a molé sauce. That would be different. Three enchiladas three ways, chicken, pork, turkey sausage, onions, garlic, poblanos, crema, cilantro sprinkled.

LALI. They slipped the tarragon in, it's like you can barely taste it but it's there.

BENG. That must be zest of an orange. So delicate.

LALI. Subtle flavors.

BENG. But muscular, like goat without goat.

> *(They eat in silence.)*

> *(Beat.)*

Scene Six

(They lie still, possibly sleeping or waiting for sleep.)

(The empty food bowl is by the transom.)

Scene Seven

*(In silence, **LALI** is giving **BENG** a windsurfing lesson for the umpteenth time. **BENG** is okay at it. **LALI** has real life experience windsurfing.)*

*(Wordlessly, she gently guides **BENG**'s body when to lean, manually adjusting **BENG**'s posture slightly.)*

(They hold the sail, knees bent, bodies bowed in matching windsurfing stances. They may barely sway, in a meditative state. It is definitely not a pantomime. Perhaps twenty to thirty seconds of silence. A temporal suspension: this is neither the beginning nor the end of the lesson.)

Scene Eight

(**LALI** *is standing like a zombie, her arms out stiffly in anticipation of a trust fall.*)

(**BENG** *stands at least three feet behind* **LALI**.)

BENG. A little less rigid.

(**LALI** *takes a breath but returns to a rigid state.*)

That's a little better.

LALI. Shut up.

BENG. No, I mean it; it was almost imperceptible, but I *percepted*.

LALI. Shut up.

(**BENG** *raises her arms behind* **LALI**, *to catch* **LALI** *when she falls backwards.*)

(**LALI** *remains vertical and still, trying to fall back, arms outstretched.*)

(*The transom slides open. Saved!*)

(**LALI** *steps out of pose. A bowl with food is shoved in.*)

(**BENG** *initiates an impromptu standoff.*)

BENG. Do it, then you can eat.

LALI. No.

BENG. Yes. I'm not giving you any until you try it.

(**BENG** *deliberately stands between the bowl of food and* **LALI**, *perhaps even repositioning herself to catch* **LALI**.)

(**LALI** *is done with the trust fall game and steps towards* **BENG** *who doesn't budge.*)

(**LALI** *steps left,* **BENG** *slides right to block her path.*)

*(**LALI** steps right, **BENG** slides left.)*

*(One more: **LALI** goes left, **BENG** slides right.)*

(Another standoff.)

(They are aware of a palpable energetic charge; an escalated friction.)

*(**LALI** wants some semblance of control and autonomy from **BENG**.)*

*(**BENG** senses **LALI**'s withholding, and tries even harder to connect.)*

(This is a new edge.)

(This goes on as long as necessary. Five seconds of silent standoff? Then:)

LALI. Grace.

BENG. Amen.

*(**LALI** takes the bowl, takes a bite and offers the bowl to **BENG**.)*

(They do not speak.)

(Beat.)

Scene Nine

*(The food bowl is gone. **LALI** is leaning over **BENG**, stretching **BENG**'s hamstrings.)*

*(**BENG**'s leg is vertical ninety degrees as **LALI** gradually pushes it down towards her face, using the weight of her own body.)*

*(Once **LALI** gets close to **BENG**'s face, **BENG** speaks.)*

BENG. Concentration camp or Gulag?

LALI. *(Yawns at **BENG**.)* Bat mitzvah or quinceañera?

BENG. ...

LALI. *(Indignant.)* What, you already did that one.

BENG. Okay, well I don't remember your answer.

LALI. Maybe you should write it down.

BENG. *(Whiny.)* But my carpal tunnel! *(Riffing, alarm.)* ...And my carpel diem!

LALI. Gulag.

BENG. Gulag.

LALI. I know.
Middle Passage or Field Slave.

BENG. Field.

LALI. Field.

BENG. Bayonet or Sword?

LALI. Bayonet.

> *(She mimes a bayonet stab, then the slash of a sword, deciding.)*

No, sword.

BENG. Sword.
Oppressor or oppressed?

LALI. Oppressor.

BENG. Oppressor.
But...*then* you'd be full of guilt.

LALI. An oblivious oppressor!

BENG. So, an American.

LALI. I'm calling a freeze on depressing thoughts or images.

BENG. I call a freeze on violence or heterosexuality.

LALI. I'm serious though. I need –

>(**LALI** *feels a strange bump on the back of* **BENG***'s upper thigh.*)

What is that?

BENG. Nothing.

>(**LALI** *goes to look,* **BENG** *pulls her leg away.*)

LALI. Show it to me.

BENG. It's a mark / from sitting.

LALI. Let me see it.

BENG. There's nothing to see.

>(**BENG** *tucks her leg under her.* **LALI** *lunges for her.*)

LALI. You got that when?

BENG. My toenail dug into my leg – a little scratch. / It's nothing.

LALI. Let me see it then.

BENG. No. It's a scratch.

LALI. Let me see it.

BENG. It was a self-inflicted accident, that's all.

LALI. How?

BENG. I was doing mule kicks and grazed my leg.

LALI. Why didn't you say something at / the time?

BENG. It didn't hurt. I didn't even notice it.

LALI. When did you / notice it?

BENG. I don't know. It's a scratch, I didn't think about it.

LALI. Didn't you feel it getting infected? There's a bump there, it's raised.

BENG. I didn't notice it. It's fine.

>(*They sit in silence.*)

(**LALI** *rolls* **BENG** *over to look at the bump.* **BENG** *pushes her off.*)

(**LALI** *withdraws immediately.* **LALI** *stares straight ahead. She is furious.*)

(**BENG** *says nothing.*)

(**LALI** *does not trust* **BENG.***)

Scene Ten

(They are still in silence.)

Scene Eleven

(**BENG** *eats from the food bowl.*)

(**LALI** *faces away.*)

(**BENG** *sets the half full food bowl down beside* **LALI** *who does not budge.*)

(*They remain in silence.*)

BENG. Come on.

(**BENG** *scoops the contents of the bowl into her palm and puts the bowl by the door.*)

(**BENG** *sits with the food in her hand on her lap and waits.*)

Scene Twelve

(**BENG** *straddles* **LALI**, *her knees pin* **LALI**'s *arms down but* **LALI**'s *mouth is shut tight. If* **LALI** *is stronger than* **BENG**, **LALI** *is using all her focus to contain her aggression towards* **BENG**, *sort of like a volcano counting to ten. If* **BENG** *is stronger than* **LALI**, *this is not a threatening stance,* **BENG** *wants her to eat because she needs to eat.*)

(*With one hand,* **BENG** *makes a sudden, desperate attempt to put the food in* **LALI**'s *closed mouth.* **BENG** *recoils quickly.* **LALI** *peels the food off her face and body and wipes it on the ground or the wall.*)

LALI. (*Volcanic.*) You don't get to win!

(**LALI** *looks at her. Something between them is confirmed, decided.*)

Scene Thirteen

(**LALI** *needs water.*)

(**BENG** *is banging on the transom and asking the door a question.*)

(**BENG** *need not be fluent in these languages, it's better if she's not a savant, but that she's been around enough to know a basic word like water in multiple languages. Her pronunciation is not perfect for the Chinese and Turkish, and she's out of practice anyway.*)

BENG. Can we please get some water?

DIALOGUE.	PRONUNCIATION.	LANGUAGE.
Biddi ma.	bid-DEE muh	Arabic
Suya ihtiyacimiz var.	s o o - Y A H ee(h)-tee-YAH-juh-MUHZ vahr	Turkish
Woda.	VWOdah	Russian
Shui.	shoo-ay	Chinese
J'ai besoin de l'eau?	jzhay beh-ZWEHN-dih loh	French
Necessito agua?	neh-SEH-see-toe AH-gwah	Spanish

WATER?

WATER!

WATER!

(**BENG** *pounds the door.*)

(*Nothing.*)

(*Silence and the sound of* **BENG**'s *breathing.*)

Scene Fourteen

> (**BENG** *is kneeling before* **LALI** *with her hands cupped at* **LALI**'s *groin as* **LALI** *pisses into* **BENG**'s *hands.*)

> (**LALI** *lowers herself to drink her own urine from* **BENG**'s *hands.*)

> (**LALI** *wipes off her face.* **BENG** *wipes off her hands on the ground.*)

BENG. How is that?

LALI. Okay.

> (*Beat.*)

> (**BENG** *risks a sommelier impression, possibly tentatively at first.*)

BENG. That was from one of our oakier barrels, we age the Chardonnays in casks for eighteen months. This one is known for having a little funk on it.

> (**BENG** *pauses briefly, perhaps assessing.*)

Sort of a barnyard funk. But I'll let you in on a little secret, which we really have to keep between us, before we soak the grapes, we run female urine through the oak barrels, it's nicknamed the douche.

> (*She pauses, then resumes.*)

It's a trick my father learned when he traveled through Greece and Turkey.

The French don't do it. They look down on it. But when France's Chardonnays were dethroned by California's, the secret was female YOO-rine (*Hard i vowel sound, rhymes with moo-mine.*).

Oh sure, they tested it with cow urine, (*Regular US pronunciation.*), weasel urine, bat guano, hamster urine, cat urine, and male human urine and overwhelmingly, the only kind that didn't poison the barrels was female YOO-rine (*British again.*).

(Pause.)

That one you tried is a good vintage. Grand Cru. You're one of the lucky ones.

(Pause.)

Fortunate to be around to taste such a vintage.

(BENG *looks at* **LALI.)**

Hang in, muffin.

LALI. Will we?

BENG. Of course.

(Beat.)

Scene Fifteen

(**BENG** *is staring ahead. She is so still she could be meditating, but she isn't.*)

(*In a full stretch in the middle of the cell,* **LALI** *comes out of a pose and bursts into running in place with high knees, alternating legs. Her hand slaps her thigh as each knee rises. It's rigorous and with each leg up she makes a staccato grunt or HA sound.*)

(**BENG** *stands up with her arms and hands out wide, her fingertips nearly touching one wall, like she's measuring her wingspan between the two walls. She can't reach the other side and eyeballs the distance on the floor where her fingertips end, and then moves to that spot to measure the rest, calculating a distance in her head.*)

(**LALI** *takes a break, hocks up a lougie to deliberately swallow it. (This is unremarkable).*)

BENG. Farthest.

(*Brief pause.*)

(**LALI** *looks up but says nothing.*)

(*She begins another round of high knee slaps and noisy exhales.*)

Can something be farther than the farthest thing?

LALI. Yes. The *thing* in that sentence is relative to whatever else is in the frame.

(*Pause.* **LALI** *continues to exercise.*)

(**BENG** *walks behind* **LALI**, *briefly imitates her knee slaps.*)

(**BENG** *reaches around and with both hands pulls* **LALI***'s hips into her own from behind.*)

I don't want that.

(*Pause.*)

Sorry.

(*Beat.*)

BENG. Have you ever stopped to consider the global time zones?

LALI. Yes.

BENG. And.

LALI. They're stupid.

BENG. That's what I was thinking. We all are in agreement of something that is *completely* illogical, but, we've agreed on it.

LALI. What are you talking about?

BENG. What are you talking about, you said they're stupid.

LALI. Because everything is stupid. You're stupid, I'm stupid.

BENG. Oh. So if I said, had you considered pancake sightings of religious figures you would have said –

LALI. Stupid.

BENG. Or gaucho pants.

LALI. Stupid.

BENG. Keratin. /

LALI. Stupid. What?

BENG. A natural polymer in your hair.

LALI. Keratin, polymer, hair, natural, stupid.

(*Silence.*)

BENG. Okay. What I was referring to is, don't you think it's weird we have all these countries around the world and we agree on almost nothing – we don't *all* have an agreement about, what, international justice, or crime and punishment?

But we agree to time zones? How did that happen?

> (**LALI** *begins doing "mountain climbers" or pushups or something as grueling.*)

Like if you were a country and you wanted to exert power, you could declare whatever your state is, print new money if you wanted, and you could also say it's now – whatever time – say, it's four o'clock and the new four o'clock is going to last three hours and fifty-three minutes and then it will be five o'clock and then nineteen minutes later I say it's now six o'clock.

> (*Pause.*)

Mostly I'm just surprised that people agree to the shit they agree to...collectively, I mean. What's the actual science behind time zones? They're completely arbitrary, are they not? ...

How could some place be exactly six hours ahead of some place else, and be exactly five hours ahead of somewhere else – that just doesn't even make sense. Temperature, I get, it's a measurable degree and it's not fixed.

> (*Pause.*)

But time. It's weird. It makes me think I'm living in some made-up land.

> (**LALI** *continues with her "mountain climbers," now counting out loud.*)

LALI. Sixteen.

Seventeen.

Eighteen.

Nineteen.

Twenty.

> (**LALI** *stops, rolls up to standing and then re-hangs, her head bent over her knees, the backs of her hands skim the ground.*)
>
> (*She coughs.*)
>
> (*She stifles a cough.*)

(She coughs again.)

BENG. Lift your head when you cough. It's bad to do it upside down.

> *(**LALI** gets her cough under control and perhaps, if she feels like it, without looking up, flips **BENG** the bird.)*

> *(**LALI** rolls up to standing.)*

> *(Pause.)*

> *(**BENG** puts her thumb and middle finger around **LALI**'s wrist, but before she can measure, **LALI** pulls her arm away.)*

LALI. If you want to touch any part of me you have to ask my permission.

> *(**BENG** nods.)*

BENG. May I touch your soul?

LALI. No.

> *(Pause.)*

BENG. Hey...

> *(**LALI** doesn't answer.)*

I said hey...?

LALI. What.

BENG. Hey can I touch your drawers.

LALI. No.

BENG. Can I touch your ego?

LALI. No.

BENG. Can I touch your sympathy?

> *(**LALI** doesn't answer. She stretches her legs, a post-running hamstrings stretch, where both hands push against the floor and her legs are extended out.)*

> *(**BENG** puts her shoulder against the floor next to where **LALI**'s hands are already pressed*

against it. **BENG** *grunts, pushing the floor with all her might.)*

I'm sorry pal, I can NOT get this sucker to move one centimeter.

(She throws herself against the floor.)

It is on there very securely.

(Wriggling in between **LALI** *and the floor.)*

It would take –

*(**LALI** *headbutts* **BENG** *hard.* **BENG** *crumples holding her head.)*

*(**BENG** *lies there, protecting her organs.)*

LALI. Just, shut up. Shut up shut up shut up shut up shut up shut up shut up.

*(**BENG** *folds herself into a turtle position, knees on the ground in a tight child's pose but with her hands folded by her head, forehead pressing into the ground.)*

BENG. I don't know what time it is.
I don't know what day or month it is.

*(**BENG** *begins to weep and weep.)*

(There's nothing for **LALI** *to say or do. So she does nothing.)*

Scene Sixteen

(**BENG**'s hands are gripping her own neck, she is choking and sputtering, **LALI**'s hands are on top of **BENG**'s holding on. It's briefly unclear if **LALI** is helping or harming **BENG**. **LALI** is trying to pry **BENG**'s hands off her neck.)

(**LALI** successfully yanks **BENG**'s hands and they lose their balance.)

(On the ground **LALI** rolls onto/over/across **BENG**, draping her own torso diagonally across **BENG**'s chest. **BENG** is subdued like a very informal straight jacket. **LALI** places her hand over **BENG**'s.)

(Adrenaline dissipating, **LALI** slides her head into the crook of **BENG**'s neck, her hand remaining across **BENG**'s body, like a sideways embrace.)

(**BENG** does not engage. It is unlike **LALI** to cling but she is.)

(**LALI** holds **BENG**.)

LALI. Please. Don't do that ever again.

(They lie still.)

I need you.

(Pause.)

BENG. I know.

(They lie still, breathing and spent.)

(The transom slides and their bowl of food is pushed in, followed by a sixteen ounce cheap plastic water bottle filled halfway with a light brown liquid. This discolored water is cause for mistrust and alarm. What is the meaning of it?)

(They are very thirsty but neither touches the bottle.)

(Beat.)

*(**BENG** reaches for the bowl, avoiding the bottle. She smells the food, it seems okay.)*

Well... Grace.

(She takes a bite, chews slowly.)

*(**LALI** sniffs.)*

Tastes the same. It seems okay...

*(**LALI** takes a small bite. It does taste the same.)*

So I guess I'll drink this...potion.

LALI. Don't.

BENG. Okay.

(They eat in silence.)

(Beat.)

LALI. What do you think?

BENG. I don't know.

Not much of a choice...

*(Pause. **BENG** looks like she might pick up the bottle.)*

LALI. Wait.

BENG. For?

LALI. Be careful.

*(**BENG** slowly opens the bottle. Sniffs hesitantly.)*

BENG. Well, it's not sewage.

*(**BENG** puts the cap on, studies the water. Pause.)*

Maybe they're tired of watching over us.

LALI. *(Perhaps to convince herself?)* That can't be.

(*The thought demoralizes her.*)

BENG. I'm trying it.

(**BENG** *pours a little liquid into her palm. She puts her tongue to her palm.*)

It doesn't taste off...

(**BENG** *takes a slow small sip and gently swishes it inside her mouth.*)

LALI. ...

BENG. (*Swishing.*) ...it could be fine, rust maybe.

Let me...?

(*She sniffs.*)

Doesn't smell.

You should wait.

LALI. For what? The sprinklers to go off? I'm fucking thirsty.

(*Beat.*)

It would be really fucking funny...if the water is fine but your hand is toxic.

(**BENG** *considers this.*)

BENG. That would be really fucking funny.

(*Pause.*)

I signed a DNR.

LALI. Noted.

BENG. And you?

LALI. Oh who the fuck cares?

(**BENG** *takes a sip of water.*)

It's probably fine.

BENG. But just in case, I would like closed casket. You?

LALI. Open, and dressed and made up like Elvis.

BENG. Costello?

LALI. Exactly.

BENG. Wake or shiva?

(**LALI** *considers.*)

LALI. Whatever people want. It's not *for* me. Let them decide.

BENG. I like the *idea* of a wake. But not in someone's home, at a zoo or a park. A big picnic. With frisbee, wiffle ball. Balloon animals, Stevie Wonder. – As a playlist, not the man himself. Although that's fine if he shows up / to boogie down.

LALI. I sort of wish I'd had a birthday party that was a funeral.

Everybody comes and give speeches about you, you get to hear how much these people love and admire you. Why not do that while you're around to hear it?

BENG. Sure.

I think we should have a wake.

Right? I mean, why not?

LALI. Poorly attended.

BENG. Okay, it's a wake, but you also have to say something about yourself, as if you were commenting on yourself. You know? The deep shit. Life. The real stuff.

LALI. Now?

BENG. No. We have to prepare what we'll say. About each other. About ourselves.

I mean, like, really say things.

LALI. Okay. I guess if I have time.

BENG. When should we do it?

LALI. Let me check my calendar. Meetings, deadlines, and the holidays and...it's nuts. I'm free later, does that work?

BENG. Yup. So many interns working, so my skedge is flex. Did I tell you I got indentured servants? – They don't tell you this when you order them, but the delegating – you have to explain *everything*, they're like puppies at first – eating your shoes and peeing in the house. (*Referring to the liquid.*) What do you think...?

LALI. I'm thirsty.
BENG. Take our chances, I guess…

Scene Seventeen

LALI. In hindsight... I think my dad was a loner.

BENG. I'm pretty sure my dad played team sports just to have people to hang out with. I don't know why he was into swimming. It's even more boring than running.

LALI. My great-aunt swam. Competitively, before that was a thing.

BENG. What was her event?

LALI. Breast stroke.

BENG. – *(Snickers.)*

LALI. What?

BENG. I didn't know if that was a pun...or...fact? Wasn't she the one with the huge / tits?

LALI. No. Wrong aunt.

BENG. Cool. She won races?

LALI. She had a bunch of medals.

BENG. That's so cool! Olympics?

LALI. No. All-county, all-state.

BENG. Still. Very impressive.

LALI. I know.

BENG. Which side, was she?

LALI. *(Like* **BENG** *is a moron.)* Dad's.

BENG. I thought. But part of me was like – I mean, maybe...?
How cool would it have been if it was your mom's side... For that time.

LALI. It wasn't progressive like that. So... no.

BENG. No, I know, I just meant...never mind. It's really cool your great-aunt was –

LALI. You bring up the Olympics, which automatically reduces whatever success she had to less – you do that...you know.

BENG. Sorry.

LALI. It doesn't matter. / But it's obnoxious

BENG. I wasn't / trying to –

LALI. It's diminishing.

BENG. It's not on purpose.
Seriously, you're bothered because I suggested your great-aunt was good enough to medal at the Olympics? That's the opposite of diminishing –

LALI. Uh, no, it's not because / automatically anything less than that is.

BENG. If I were to say oh, hey, did your little lady aunt get a medal at the town fair for swimming, well that would be / diminishing – low expectations.

LALI. Never mind. You don't get it.

BENG. *You* don't get it! You cast your / shadow on what I say and then – I don't know,

LALI. Drop it, I don't / care to –

BENG. Pin something uh small-minded or / whatever on me.

LALI. Just never mind. /

BENG. I'm not apologizing for something I didn't / do.

LALI. Fine.

BENG. I'm retracting the apology I gave a moment ago.
And... I actually think you might want to consider looking at your own uh, assumptions and maybe commenting on that to me. As in, an apology.

LALI. I'm not. I mean, I'm... no.

> (**BENG** *sighs a "you're in the wrong" sigh.*)

> (*They are silent.*)

> (**BENG** *does a weird move where she dives onto the ground like a breakdancer – not as showy, not as smooth. She executes a fake dive and lowers to the ground.*)

> (**BENG***'s chin and head are slightly arched, the rest of her body rests on the ground.*)

(She begins to kick her feet and move her right arm in an unpracticed crawl stroke.)

*(**BENG** adds her left arm. She is athletic but doesn't stroke well. Also, she's on the ground so it's very much not the same as swimming.)*

BENG. I'm basically shit at swimming.

*(**LALI** approaches **BENG** and holds her head – adjusts it as if **BENG** is underwater but **LALI** is holding the weight of **BENG**'s head. **BENG** draws her right hand back, and **LALI** lifts **BENG**'s head.)*

LALI. That's when you breathe, at the start of the stroke. When this hand comes down, your head is already under and you can glide.

BENG. Oh. So, let me –

*(**BENG** does it with her left arm stroke and lifts her head.)*

LALI. Fingers like this...

BENG. Do I just breathe on the one side?

LALI. Both sides.

*(**LALI** lies on the ground and swims.)*

*(**BENG** watches **LALI** a moment then starts to swim too.)*

(They swim on the ground next to each other.)

*(**BENG** stops, as if reaching the lip of a pool and pretends to remove her goggles.)*

BENG. These gogglers leak.

*(As if resting her arms on the lip of the pool, **BENG** folds her hands and rest her chin atop, looking out.)*

Ahhhhhhhhhhh.

LALI. I'm in freshwater. 'Lac's Pond.

BENG. I just popped into the "Y" on my lunch break.

LALI. I'm on vacay with my family. I love it here, we've been coming here for years. Used to be a great rope swing by that elm.

I'll tell you something funny – my cousin died – too young, in his late twenties, of cancer...we sprinkled his ashes at 'Lac's Pond.

BENG. Sorry about your cousin. You've never mentioned him.

LALI. He was on my dad's side, technically, a second cousin I guess. Men die very young on my dad's side, sort of freakishly.

BENG. I have an aversion to swampy lake bottoms. I would wear booties.

LALI. Of course you would. I prefer salt water to chlorine, but I like freshwater.

BENG. Of course you do. And I like the predictability of chlorine.

(**LALI** *stops swimming.*)

LALI. When my mom was really little, my grandmother took her into the ocean, over her head and let go.

BENG. For a split second?

LALI. No, fully let go of her. She told my mom to swim to her. My mom thinks she was maybe two. She did swim.

BENG. Just to teach her to swim?

LALI. Initially, it was probably a survival thing, that over generations became a ritual, like you did it to protect your daughter from harm.

BENG. By letting her almost drown.

LALI. No one ever did.

BENG. That you know of...

LALI. That side of the family had some good superstitions. Like you have to slit a chicken's throat left to right. Don't lock the door if *you're home.*

BENG. Did your mom do the drowning thing to you?

LALI. No. But also we were in Chicago by then.

BENG. Lake Michigan...?

LALI. Not in February. Plus, it's not the same – this was a
ritual.

BENG. Maybe that's why you like swimming.

LALI. Why.

BENG. It's part of your heritage to commune with water.

(*Silence.*)

LALI. Are you, like, preparing for the wake?

BENG. Yes. Thinking about what I'll say.
I wanted to ask you – I guess, if you think – well, what
the parameters are, around – you know, other people?

LALI. Would you like to involve them?

BENG. Um, invoke, maybe? I don't know. It feels like we
can't *not*, but at the same time...it's kind of...maybe...
destabilizing? I mean, I think, I guess we should
discuss it first, and come to a decision. Like...

(*Thinking.*)

Okay, I would like to include names.

LALI. Okay. I think that's reasonable.

BENG. Are you going to?

LALI. I wasn't planning to...but. I was thinking we wouldn't,
just, I guess the rules, but... I don't know... I –

BENG. But also, I mean, I could and you could not... You
know? It doesn't have to be because one does, we both
do. And, I guess my question is, *if* we use names, are
we inviting them in?

LALI. And speaking...

BENG. Yes.

LALI. Oh. Uhhhhhm. I don't know.

(*They both think.*)

What do you want?

BENG. What do you want?

LALI. I don't know. I'm – well, at this point I'm sort of having second thoughts on the whole thing.

BENG. Oh.

LALI. I think it's maybe not a good idea. In a – deeply subcutaneous kind of way. Like unsubconsciously.

BENG. What does that mean...to you?

LALI. Basically, it's Pandora-ish. The first thought I had, when you said the names was the – you know the Jewish giant guy they created –

BENG. Yes, his um, he's a, he's a giant, made from the earth –

LALI. Clay. He's called a Gollom. / No – a – um –

BENG. *Gollum* is the / one from –

LALI. I know, I didn't mean – I – Go-lem. Go-lum?

BENG. That sounds right, GO-lum.

LALI. It's spelled G-O-L-E-M. Go-lem. The Jews made him out of clay to save them – their village, they're gonna be killed – he saves them from death / and destruction.

BENG. *(Excitedly.)* He's a monster and they've made him and they can't – am I mixing Judaica with the legend of Frankenstein? / I thought I remember, he can't go back into the earth once...

LALI. It's something like that – I don't think it's that, but I think it's about creating something out of the need to be saved, and it works, but then there are consequences / to that.

BENG. I wasn't going to build a GO-lum. I don't think I'm Jewish enough.

LALI. Or at all.

BENG. I've been to Seders. Bar mitzvahs. Bahhht mitzvahs.

LALI. You've also gone to Quaker meetings, that doesn't / make you –

BENG. You don't have to convert to Quakerism. Can't you just go to meetings and be one?

LALI. I don't know.

BENG. The Mormons claim people from other faiths posthumously.

LALI. Yes I know.

BENG. That's such lazy proselytizing. It's cheating.

LALI. It reflects poorly on the Tabernacle.

>*(Beat.)*

If you want to use names, I'm cool with it.

BENG. And if you want to...

LALI. Yeah. I don't know.

>*(Pause.)*

But, I guess I somehow...

...I'd like to propose that we are not to speak as anyone but ourselves.

BENG. Okay. And we still each speak at each other's?

LALI. Yes.

BENG. Okay.

LALI. Hey, would you sing something at mine?

BENG. Like what?

LALI. I don't know. Something fitting. Whatever you think of that feels right... Thank you.

BENG. I haven't sung in a long time though. My voice is probably...not great.

LALI. It's okay, I'll be dead, so there's no judgment.

Scene Eighteen

(**BENG** *is alone in the cell. She sits very still (listening).)*

(Time passes.)

Scene Nineteen

(**BENG** *is alone in the cell, soothing herself. Maybe rocking, or holding the floor.*)

Scene Twenty

(**BENG** *is alone. She is singing Irving Berlin's "After You Get What You Want You Don't Want It" perhaps in preparation for* **LALI**'s *wake.*)

BENG.
AFTER YOU GET WHAT YOU WANT, YOU DON'T WANT IT
IF I GAVE YOU THE MOON, YOU'D GROW TIRED OF IT
   SOON

YOU'RE LIKE A BABY
YOU WANT WHAT YOU WANT WHEN YOU WANT IT

   (*Hums, or forgets, skips and picks up.*)

YOU'RE ALWAYS WISHING AND WANTING FOR
   SOMETHING
WHEN YOU GET WHAT YOU WANT
YOU DON'T WANT WHAT YOU GET

   (*Hums, skips and picks up.*)

'CAUSE AFTER YOU GET WHAT YOU WANT
YOU DON'T WANT WHAT YOU WANTED / AT ALL

   (*She has a coughing fit.*)

Scene Twenty-One

(**BENG** *is on her back, feet in the air, as a tired waiter or construction worker might rest.*)

(**LALI** *is entirely clean, but wearing the same cotton shift as before.*)

(*Eventually, she goes and sits by* **BENG**.)

(**LALI** *extends her hand, as an offering.*)

(**BENG** *rests her head in* **LALI**'s *hand.*)

Scene Twenty-Two

(**LALI** *is curled in a ball, her side against the ground.*)

(**BENG** *puts a hand on* **LALI**'*s shoulder, testing.*)

(**LALI** *nods.*)

(*Gradually* **BENG** *moves her entire body next to* **LALI**'*s, spooning her.*)

(**LALI** *weeps.*)

(**BENG** *holds her.*)

(**BENG** *slowly approaches* **LALI**'*s feet and begins to massage or lightly tickle them.* **BENG** *begins at* **LALI**'*s feet and playfully sniffs* **LALI**, *a tender, full-body sniff which* **LALI** *allows. It's a delicious feeling and* **LALI** *laughs.* **BENG** *catches it.*)

(*They laugh really hard.*)

Scene Twenty-Three

LALI. Did you ever take one of those Meyers-Briggs tests?

BENG. No. I don't like personality or EQ or introvert or any of those tests. Why?

LALI. Wondering. I never did either.

BENG. They seem – unimaginative. Maybe even harmful… Oh you're *this person* so you're likely to think and behave *this way*. Maybe you start to behave and think that way because it's what's expected of you. I feel that way about astrology.

The horoscopes… I could *be* an Aries just as much as I could *not be* an Aries.

  (Pause.)

LALI. You're not an Aries.

BENG. Yeah I am.

LALI. Your birthday is April 22.

BENG. That's Aries. / The edge, I guess.

LALI. No. That's a Taurus.

BENG. Are / you – *(Sure.)*

LALI. YES.

BENG. Oh. I could still *be* an Aries just as much as I could *not* be an Aries. That's how useless it is: I thought I was an Aries and now I'm not. Who cares…?

LALI. A lot of people find significance in it. Doesn't mean you have to.

  (Silence.)

BENG. Do you still want to do the wakes?

LALI. Not really.

  (Pause.)

BENG. I would like to.

LALI. You can do yours.

BENG. Will you say something?

LALI. If you want me to.

BENG. I do.

>*(Pause.)*

I'd like to do mine now. Do you need any more time to prepare anything?

LALI. *(Thinks. She does that tapping with her tongue on the roof of her mouth habit.)* How long is whatever you're saying?

BENG. I don't know...not that long. I have some things. I'm gonna improvise.

It's okay if yours is short – or, you know, brief.

Don't feel like you have to.

LALI. Okay.

BENG. Okay what?

LALI. Okay, I'm ready.

BENG. You sure?

LALI. Yes.

BENG. Okay.

Um, I'm using my *(Touching her shift.)* ...as me.

So, we'll just, I guess, start?

LALI. Okay. How do you want this to go?

>*(**BENG** removes her shift and lays it out on the floor.)*

>*(She chooses where to stand and begins, as if addressing guests on three sides of her.)*

BENG. Today we mourn the passing of Beatrix Norman Grey. It is neither a sad occasion, nor a joyous one, for we are united in mourning and loss.

We are aware of the grace that comes from being here together.

If we look into our hearts, there is a place in each of us, in which we loved something of her, some part that was like us, or something we identified with, or yearned for...or even hated, in that way that we hate the thing we love the most.

(She halts abruptly.)

Now, we will hear from someone who knew her in a way that no one else could. They were kept for a time in a small cell.

*(**BENG** steps back.)*

*(**LALI** steps forward.)*

LALI. I have never met anyone like Beatrix Norman Grey. It would not suffice to say I loved her, although I did, deeply. As one loves a sister, a mother or a lover.

BENG. Or all three.

LALI. Do not heckle. This is by request.

BENG. Not too formal.

LALI. I said twelve words, / three were your name!

BENG. Try telling an anecdote...

LALI. Okay. One you have in mind?

BENG. Up to you.

LALI. Okay.

Apparently, Beatrix and I first met at a New Year's party, but neither of us remembered meeting the other. Except, once we figured out we were both there, Beng *insisted* she *did* remember and told me *exactly* what I wore.

She was wrong. I didn't own a green dress, black *high* heels?! No. She wanted to bet money on it. She was so stubborn. Must have been the Taurus in her.

Years later, I actually saw a photo from that party. She was right. I had *borrowed* that dress and shoes.

BENG. You're not doing it right.

LALI. *You said* anec / dote.

BENG. This is like a roast – it's supposed to be a commemoration / of a life.

LALI. Okay – / I'm sorry.

BENG. Or don't / do it.

LALI. I'm trying. I haven't done this before, I don't know how –

BENG. You've been to a wake.

LALI. Yes. Okay.

Do you prefer Beatrix / or Beng?

BENG. Beng is fine.

LALI. Beng and I met as colleagues some years after that New Year's party, on an airplane. Takeoff was delayed, I was on my first overseas gig, I was very much the rookie, visibly nervous and sweating.

In the seat in front of me, sat Beng, looking seasoned and cool, and like effortlessly beautiful… I remember wanting to know her, and wanting to find out, was she ever not confident? She knew a little about a lot and she knew a lot about a lot. She worked hard. She was thoughtful and…just very human – in the best and deepest meaning of the word. She had her longings and yearnings, like any of us.

She was generous and genuine.

I think there was sort of a hidden part of her, that was maybe frozen at thirteen, still unsure of her place in the world. She told great stories – although at times she could misread her audience… Oh, she could be judgmental, argumentative, and competitive…over the smallest things.

But she got away with it because she radiated warmth – she carried it in her eyes, her hands, jaw, her feet, her cowlick.

She gave the best foot massages, better than Chinese masseuses.

When…we were captives…and she held me…in her arms, with my head nestled into the crook of her neck, that became home.

If not for Beng… I would not stand here today.

She saved my life. She literally kept me alive.

I miss her already.

And I celebrate her, for she is free.

(**LALI** *steps away.*)

(**BENG** *steps forward, fussing with the shift.*)

BENG. There are a few words I would like to say about Beng. She didn't let on but she was afraid much of her life. That she wouldn't amount to her potential.

Irony was, no one had expected much of her, they were surprised when she finished high school on time. What they assumed is she'd find a job, get married and have four kids. Live down the street or at most across town, and celebrate birthdays and anniversaries with her family. When she finished university, her parents stood at the back of the gymnasium holding helium balloons. Her older brothers were working.

She did marry. She left her. She came back. She left her. She came back, and one day she left her. Left all of it. She thought she could be somebody she would admire / but –

LALI. You're making a mockery out of this thing that you wanted to do.

BENG. I'm boring.

LALI. I know. Boring is where the meat is.

BENG. She never felt like she was capable of loving another person or of being lovable. She chose women who were unavailable and pursued them, and when she got one, she'd find her way out.

Raising a child was the hardest thing she ever tried. And she wasn't good at it. She's so sorry. She made a lot of mistakes. She hopes she is forgiven…

She wanted to be someone who other people couldn't resist loving.

She desperately wanted to love unconditionally.

She died for your sins. Rest in peace.

> (**BENG** *lies facing down, matching her arms with the arms and torso of her shift. Arms out, she may resemble a post-crucifixion Christ.*)

Scene Twenty-Four

(**BENG** *is alone in the cell, wearing her same shift, listening by the transom.*)

(*She hears what might be music, faintly. It could be African Highlife music, Bollywood pop, strains of 70s British disco*? **BENG** can't place it.*)

(*Whatever it was stops.*)

(*Silence.*)

(*Beat.*)

(**BENG** *backs away from the transom. She hocks up a loogie in her mouth. She waits.*)

---

* A license to produce *No One Is Forgotten* does not include a performance license for any third-party or copyrighted music. Licensees should create an original composition or use music in the public domain. For further information, please see Music Use Note on page 3.

Scene Twenty-Five

(**BENG** *and* **LALI** *are together in the cell.*)

(*They are not speaking.*)

(**BENG** *slowly approaches. Her voice is strange.*)

BENG. Can I sit beside you?

(**LALI** *says nothing, but it's apparent to* **BENG** *she may sit.*)

(*They sit in silence.*)

What do you think they will do to me?

(**LALI** *says nothing.*)

Can I hold your hand?

(**BENG** *slowly curls entirely around* **LALI** *who remains sitting.*)

(**BENG** *is loosely spooning, as close as she can get without* **LALI** *pushing her away.*)

If you don't touch me, I think I will really die.

LALI. You won't.

BENG. I want to die.

LALI. Just think of Thomas.

BENG. I can't. I don't care anymore. I can't.

LALI. Connie, Thomas, Adam, Jeanette, Stephen, Charles, Charles Junior, Monica, Jenny, Franklin.

(**BENG** *cries.*)

BENG. I don't care.

LALI. Say it with me.

BENG. –

LALI. Connie. Thomas.

(*Pause.*)

Adam. Jeanette. Stephen.

BENG. Stephen.

    (Together:)

LALI. Charles, Charles Junior. Monica. Jenny. Franklin.

BENG. Charles, Charles Junior. Monica. Jenny. Franklin.

LALI. Connie... Thomas...

BENG. –   – ...

Scene Twenty-Six

> (**LALI** *and* **BENG** *have been given two bowls of food and two wooden spoons, for the first time. They are cautious, and hungry. They are taking small bites from each bowl and swapping bowls between them, a means of being equally at risk.*)

LALI. It doesn't taste different.

BENG. But why two bowls? Spoons?

LALI. ... (*How would I know?*)

BENG. You don't think it's thicker?

LALI. I don't. No. What do you want to do?

BENG. I just don't know if we should eat it.

LALI. Okay.

> (*They stop eating.*)

> (*Pause.*)

BENG. Maybe this is our last meal.
What if they listened to the wake and – they know I want to die.

LALI. Scale of one to five, if dying is five and sitting here is one, where are you?

BENG. 4.79999.

LALI. Beng.

BENG. I feel guilty. If you weren't here it would be a solid five.

LALI. I'm only worth .21 to you?

BENG. (*Deeply honest.*) You're worth an incalculable amount.

> (*Silence.*)

LALI. How come you don't ask me?

BENG. What? Oh, sorry. One to five?

LALI. Well... Three is the median.

BENG. Not necessarily – if you're at one and five an equal amount, then yes.

LALI. I can't remember the fucking difference between median and average!

I was good at statistics! I understood graphs – now I can't recall shit and it feels ridiculous to eat with a spoon.

BENG. Our minds rot! Without nutrition! The stuff we *think* keeps our minds active isn't / enough!

LALI. We should do more!

BENG. It's not our fault!

LALI. What is the point of that – what does fault have to do with / anything?!

BENG. That we can't exercise our brains, not enough nutrients is not our fault.

That's ALL I WAS SAYING.

LALI. I HOPE THIS <u>IS</u> POISONED!

> (**LALI** *eats out of the bowl with her hand.*)

> (**BENG** *eats out of* **LALI***'s bowl too.*)

> (**BENG** *adds her food to* **LALI***'s bowl, mixing it.*)

> (**LALI** *puts* **BENG***'s food back in* **BENG***'s bowl.*)

If only one bowl is poisoned I hope it's mine.

> (**BENG** *grabs* **LALI***'s bowl from her.* **LALI** *knocks the bowls out of* **BENG***'s hands. Food spills. They don't know which bowl is which.*)

> (**LALI** *takes both bowls and mixes it all together, adding whatever is on the ground.*)

> (**LALI** *gives one of the bowls to* **BENG** *and throws the spoon at her.*)

Bon appétit.

BENG. (*Raising the bowl.*) Salud.

> (*They eat in silence.*)

(**BENG** *sighs noticeably.*)

(*Silence. They eat slowly.*)

It's probably fine. (*Pause.*) We'll be old women here.

(*They eat in silence.*)

(**LALI** *has a knotting, cramped, twisted feeling on her right side, which begins as discomfort and becomes painful. Is this what poisoning feels like? No. Maybe?*)

(**BENG** *observes her.*)

Your stomach?

LALI. Yeh.

BENG. On both sides?

LALI. Right.

BENG. A dull cramp or a sharp, stabbed-in-the-gut pain?

LALI. No. Like somebody braided my intestines into a rope and *yanked*.

BENG. I told you not to do so many lunges.

LALI. Not helpful. (*Some pain.*) Lunges are legs. So.

BENG. But the psoas...? Isn't it the longest / muscle?

LALI. Psoas is your hips, pelvis, legs or sciatica in your lower back.

BENG. Maybe it will help if I rub it, like un-knot it –

LALI. / No.

BENG. Squeeze your temples / pressure points.

LALI. Just – nothing – give me space! (*To herself.*) Jesus.

(**BENG** *retreats to the farthest corner.*)

(*Pause.*)

What are you doing?

BENG. (*With an echo.*) I'm giving you space...space...space...
space...
Can you hear me...hear me...hear me...?

LALI. You're an asshole.

   (**LALI** *is interrupted by a jolt of dull pain.*)

BENG. See, / shouldn't insult people.

LALI. Now it's like a – vise.

BENG. It could be gas...but still really painful.

   (*Silence.*)

LALI. It's like being squeezed or punched – if this *is* poison, just let me fucking die / already.

BENG. I'll be so fucking pissed if you got all the poison! Should you vomit?

I think you should. Just try.

   (**LALI** *tries to make herself throw up. She only gags.*)

Put your fingers / down further?

LALI. I'm trying. /

BENG. I know, I / just mean...

LALI. Don't third base coach me –

   (**LALI** *dry heaves, gags.*)

BENG. That's it, good, / almost there...

   (*She spits. Maybe at* **BENG**'*s foot. Coughs.*)

Do not die / that's not an option.

LALI. Stop! It's a cramp or stitch. I'm not dying. / I can't handle you freaking out –

BENG. You can't leave me here.

   (**LALI** *gets into a fetal position.*)

Does that help?

LALI. No.

BENG. Want me to stroke your head?

LALI. No. Thank you. It's okay.

BENG. I don't like you in pain. I'd like to be helpful.

LALI. Just being here is fine.

BENG. Not like I'm going out for wings.

LALI. Shhh.

BENG. Sorry. I'll sit quietly. Just say if you need something.

> (**LALI** *lies there.* **BENG** *sits.*)

LALI. Can you smell the bowl?

BENG. No.

LALI. No I mean, will you smell the bowl?

BENG. Oh. Okay.

> (**BENG** *smells both bowls.*)

> (**BENG** *smells her inner elbow (clears the nasal palate) and sniffs again.*)

I think it smells...off?

LALI. Off how?

BENG. I want to say putrid, but that's not – it's more like – do you want to smell it?

LALI. No. Obviously.

BENG. No – to make you puke?

LALI. Oh. Okay.

> (**BENG** *brings the bowls to* **LALI** *and they smell them.*)

Cheese?

> (**BENG** *sniffs it again.*)

BENG. I don't smell anything. Maybe it's fermented –

LALI. Fruit?

BENG. I don't know.

LALI. Oh! I bet it *is* dairy? If I became lactose intolerant – when you don't have something, your body can reject it / when you have it.

BENG. But wouldn't I have the same –

LALI. Not everyone is lactose intolerant.

> (**LALI** *stretches out from being curled.*)

BENG. *(Vigilant.)* I'd move slowly, if / at all.

LALI. I'm seeing if moving feels any / better.

BENG. Okay. Does it?

LALI. I don't know. Stop asking me. Yes.

>*(Silence.)*

>*(**LALI** takes a slow, deep breath. And then another.)*

>*(**BENG** is trying to think of other things.)*

>Okay... I think it passed.

>*(Beat.)*

BENG. Do you think if we took ecstasy in here it could be a positive experience? Like, hug the ground, see constellations on the ceiling...sex would be...an orchestra of sound and light?

LALI. I don't know. I never took X. Or mushrooms.

BENG. But you took Ayahuasca.

LALI. That was for a spiritual journey.

BENG. X is a spiritual journey.

LALI. No, X is a party drug.

BENG. LSD was intended for research on couples.

LALI. I want seltzer with lime...

BENG. I've been craving grilled cheese! My mom would slice up garlic in the pan so it was crunchy – is it grill cheese or grillED cheese? Grilled cheese. Grill cheese.

LALI. Grilled cheese. It's a verb.

BENG. Do you actually grill it? Right? Just in a pan or a toaster oven.

LALI. A toaster oven grills it.

BENG. And I want french fries and a cool pickle.

LALI. What makes a pickle cool?

BENG. Sunglasses.

LALI. Stupid.

BENG. I know, I meant refrigerated.

LALI. You know what, I bet I can't eat ice cream...

BENG. You just take Lactaid pills. Vivi was lactose intolerant.

LALI. She was more than lactose in / tolerant.

BENG. She was just intolerant.

Maybe it was my fault.

LALI. Maybe you two should have taken LSD.

> (**LALI** *rubs her belly, as if checking to see if the pain is really gone.*)

It's better.

BENG. Want me to?

LALI. Okay.

BENG. Gentle.

> (**BENG** *begins a light massage of* **LALI***'s belly.*)

Is that good?

LALI. Yeh.

BENG. Good.

LALI. Sorry, if you thought I was mad.

> (**BENG** *reaches up and kisses the top of* **LALI***'s head and is about to sit back down when* **LALI** *takes* **BENG***'s hand with a surprising tenderness.* **LALI** *reaches for* **BENG***, initiating by pulling* **BENG** *onto her.*)

> (*They don't take their eyes off each other, as they slip their underwear off, shimmy their shifts up and fuck, bodies pressed against each other. This time, it's really intimate, eye contact, their familiarity with one another's bodies, the love they share is palpable. They are interrupted when the transom slides open.*)

> (*The transom slides open and they immediately separate.*)

> (*But no bowl, no bottle of water appears in their cell.*)

(They watch the door, what's happening? A mistake? A delay?)

(There's not been a time when nothing is delivered.)

Scene Twenty-Seven

(The room is empty, save the bucket.)

(No humans.)

(No bowl.)

(No spoons.)

(No bottle with brown liquid.)

(Beat.)

Scene Twenty-Eight

*(Alone, **LALI** is doing a walking meditation, maybe in rows or around the cell. She may walk slowly, but her speech is not slowed.)*

(She is saying goodbye to the people she loves. When she imagines some of them missing her, it is too much to bear. She wants desperately to free herself from the rage and despair she carries.)

(This is an act of reaching for self-forgiveness, of preparing for an end, and of offering a blessing.)

LALI. *(She is mid-meditation.)* ...she experience happiness and relief from all suffering.

I wish goodness to Laura. May she experience happiness and relief from all suffering.

I wish goodness to Audre. May she experience happiness and relief from all suffering.

I wish goodness to Omar, may he experience happiness and relief from all suffering.

I wish goodness to Keer, may he experience happiness and relief from all suffering.

I wish goodness to Simon, may he experience happiness and relief from all suffering.

I wish goodness to Gerald, may he experience happiness and relief from all suffering.

I wish goodness to Janice, may she experience happiness and relief from all suffering.

I wish goodness to the people I went to school with from kindergarten to college, may they all be free from all suffering and be happy.

I wish goodness to people on the street who have nowhere to live, may they experience happiness and shelter and be free from all suffering.

I wish goodness to people I have wronged, may they experience happiness and be free from all suffering.

I wish goodness to my captors, may they experience happiness... *(She pauses.)* ...and be free *(She pauses.)* from all sufferi –

> *(She cannot say it. She recommences with the familiar.)*

I wish goodness to Will. May he experience happiness and relief from all suffering.

I wish goodness to Beng. May she experience happiness and be free from all suffering.

> *(She stops her walking meditation. Not quite an afterthought.)*

I wish goodness to myself. May I experience happiness and be free from all suffering.

> *(Pause.)*

> (**LALI** *begins to walk slowly without speaking.)*

Scene Twenty-Nine

(On the ground by the transom are an untouched full bowl and spoon.)

*(**LALI** is on the ground staring up at the ceiling or imagined sky, chanting to herself.)*

LALI. Om Mata, Om Kali
Om Mata, Om Kali,
Om Mata, Om Kali,
Om Mata, Om Kali

Scene Thirty

(The bowl and spoon are gone.)

*(**LALI** removes her shift and lays it out on the floor.)*

LALI. Nicole Laleña Miller...lived a too brief life. She was a good person. She tried to be generous. She was a really loyal friend. She wanted to save lives, leave the world better than how she found it...always. She liked to be far from home. She was a wanderer, a nomad.

She is survived by a really loving family. Her father, mother, two brothers and older sister, three aunts, four uncles, twelve cousins, five nieces and two nephews. Maybe more. She leaves behind a husband, Will –

(She stops here and cannot continue.)

Will.

She died without a purpose, without ever saving a life. She died alone.

Will.

She died free. She forgave. She died unafraid of death, unafraid of life.

(Beat.)

(She decides to chant or the chant decides she should chant, either way, she will allow the words and feelings to release her from her suffering.)

(Chanting.)

(1.)

Om Mata Om Kali,
Durga Devi Namo Namaha
Shakti Kundalini,
Durga Devi Mata
Om Mata Om Kali,
Durga Devi Namo Namaha

Shakti Kundalini,
Jagadambe Mata

> (**LALI** *begins to open. Energy courses through as she channels something greater – earth, spirit, soul – is filling the room. There is no set rhythm. The vibe is all-encompassing.*)

(2.)
Om Mata Om Kali,
Durga Devi Namo Namaha
Shakti Kundalini,
Durga Devi Mata
Om Mata Om Kali,
Durga Devi Namo Namaha
Shakti Kundalini,
Jagadambe Mata

> (*She is opening further, expanding.*)

(3.)
Om Mata Om Kali,
Durga Devi Namo Namaha
Shakti Kundalini,
Durga Devi Mata
Om Mata Om Kali,
Durga Devi Namo Namaha
Shakti Kundalini,
Jagadambe Mata

> (*She is the words, the words are her. She is present and not. The room is likely gone.*)

(4.)
Om Mata Om Kali,
Durga Devi Namo Namaha
Shakti Kundalini,
Durga Devi Mata
Om Mata Om Kali,

Durga Devi Namo Namaha
Shakti Kundalini,
Jagadambe Mata

Scene Thirty-One

(**LALI** *and* **BENG** *sit together in silence in the cell.*)

(*The light moves from imperceptibly dimmer and slowly dims until near darkness.*)

(**LALI** *lies on the ground,* **BENG** *lies perpendicular to her. Her head rests on* **LALI***'s stomach.*)

(*They may or may not be holding hands.*)

BENG. Clawed apart by a bear.

LALI. Trapped under a building.

BENG. Nibbled at by ants.

(*Microbeat.*)

LALI. Tortured.

BENG. Violated.

LALI. Starved.

BENG. Forgotten.

(*Microbeat.*)

LALI. Prayed for.

BENG. Together.

LALI. Yes.

(*A long pause. They remain still.*)

(*The door opens wide into the room, sunlight from beyond the doorway pours in.*)

(*Is this freedom or violence?*)

(*Blackout.*)

End of Play